D0726683

# Ed's Funny
# Feet

Eoin Colfer

Illustrated by Woody

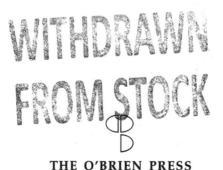

**THE O'BRIEN PRESS**
DUBLIN

First published 2000 by The O'Brien Press Ltd.,
20 Victoria Road, Dublin 6, Ireland.
Tel. +353 1 4923333; Fax. +353 1 4922777
E-mail books@obrien.ie
Website www.obrien.ie

ISBN: 0-86278-650-9

British Library Cataloguing-in-Publication Data.
A catalogue reference for this title is available from the
British Library.

1   2   3   4   5   6   7   8   9   10
00   01   02   03   04   05   06   07

The O'Brien Press receives
assistance from

**The Arts Council**
An Chomhairle Ealaíon

Layout and design: The O'Brien Press Ltd.
Illustrations: Woody
Colour separations: C&A Print Services Ltd.
Printing: Cox & Wyman Ltd.

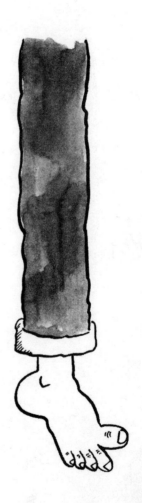

## CHAPTER 1

# Special Shoes

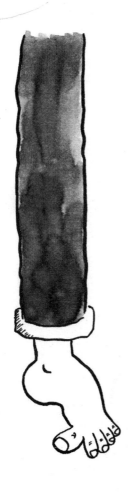

Ed Cooper had a problem with his **big toes**. They were pointing at each other instead of straight ahead.

This meant that sometimes Ed fell over when he was running.

After a while, Ed's knees were covered with so many bruises that they looked like two angry **rain clouds**.

Mum took him to see Doctor
Bert.

Ed was a little frightened.
Usually when people said
'**hmmm**', they were worried
about something.

'Hmmm,' said Doctor Bert again. 'Ed's feet are turned in.'

Ed swallowed. That sounded serious.

Doctor Bert tapped Ed's toes with a rubber hammer. 'We're going to have to straighten these little fellows out.'

Straighten them out? thought Ed. How did you straighten toes out? His Dad, a carpenter, straightened out old nails with a pair of **pliers**.

Ed hoped Doctor Bert wouldn't
be using the same tool.

Mum noticed Ed's scared face. 'Don't be afraid, Ed,' she said.

'There's no need to be afraid,' agreed Doctor Bert. 'Straightening toes doesn't **hurt** a bit.'

Doctor Bert took out a special foot measurer from a drawer.

'Now, Ed. Put your foot in here and we'll take a few measurements.'

'Measurements for what?' asked Ed.

Doctor Bert pulled the strap tight. 'Why for your correction shoes of course.'

Correction shoes? That was terrible news. Ed had heard about those. They had thick soles like planks of wood. And they were **really** old-fashioned.

## CHAPTER 2

# For your own Good

'It's for your own good,' said
Mum.

That didn't make Ed feel any
better. **Horrible** things were
always for your own good. Like
coming in out of the rain, or
going to bed early, or correction
shoes.

'No one will even notice you're wearing them.'

Ed laughed.

Mum didn't realise how important shoes were in school.
All his friends would be wearing the latest trainers.

'**Everyone** will notice, Mum!' he wailed. 'Even the baby infants won't play with me.'

Ed had two weeks until his special shoes were ready.

He decided to wear his trainers as much as possible in that time. He wore them to school, he wore them in bed, and once he even wore them in the shower!

Mum was **not**
very pleased when
she found the whole house
covered with soggy footprints.

Fourteen days later, the shoes arrived ...

The box they came in was plain brown without any bright colours, explosions or even a few stripes.

Ed was worried. Even the **box** was old-fashioned.

Mum cut the string and peeled off the tissue paper. They peered in together.

The shoes were nothing like he'd imagined ...

They were **worse**!

Ed had painted a picture in his mind of big, black shoes like Grandad's. These were more like toddlers' sandals – with **baby buckles**! And thick, white soles.

Ed had to get
away as **fast** as
he could.
He turned and
raced up the
stairs, imagining
the special shoes
running after
him. He didn't
feel safe until the
bedroom door
was locked.

He put his ear to the door and listened. Were the shoes out there?

Waiting for him to creep out? Then they would pounce on his feet and **never** let go!

Ed lay on his bed and thought. He needed a plan. He closed his eyes and waited for one to pop into his head. After sixteen minutes he had an idea. He would make a **do-it-yourself** foot straightener.

## CHAPTER 3

# Do-it-Yourself

'Come out of there!' shouted Ed's
Mum through the keyhole.

'I can't,' Ed shouted back. 'I'm inventing.'

'Well invent quickly,' said Mum. 'Dinner will be ready in half an hour.'

Ed searched his drawers for foot-straightening equipment.
The straightest things he could find were a ruler, two pencils, a frisbee and a purple crayon.

**Perfect**.

Ed took off his trainers and socks. He sellotaped the frisbee and the crayon to one foot, and the pencils and ruler to the other.

**That** should do the trick.

Ed walked up and down the room. With every step, he stamped his foot to give the straighteners a hand. It was difficult to walk with a **frisbee** stuck to your foot.

After eighty-five trips across
the room, the crayon broke. A few
trips later, the pencils snapped.

Ed sighed. His foot-
straighteners were worn out.
Time to check the **results**.

ouch!

Ed sat on the bed and unwound
the sellotape. He looked at his toes,
and his toes wiggled back at him.
They were the **very** same, not one bit
straighter. His invention hadn't
worked.

'Ed!' called his mother. 'Finish off inventing and come down. Dinner is ready!'

Ed thought about keeping the door locked,  but he was hungry and he didn't like fighting with Mum. So he opened the door.

The correction shoes were on the landing – waiting for him. They seemed to **watch** him with their baby buckles.

Ed jumped over the correction shoes and ran down the stairs.

He **nearly** made it to the bottom too. But, at the second last step, his toes tripped him. He rolled along the carpet and banged his knee against the wall.

It didn't hurt very much, but Ed felt like hitting the wall. So he did.

## CHAPTER 4

# Picking Teams

On Monday, Ed had to try on the shoes. They felt **strange**, as though he were standing on two bricks. His feet felt crooked, even though the shoes were supposed to straighten them out.

Mum dropped him to school.

'Right then, honey,' she said, kissing him on the cheek. 'Off you go.'

Ed didn't go **anywhere**.

'My stomach hurts,' he said.

Mum put her arm around him. 'Does it really?'

'No,' said Ed. 'I just don't want to go to school.'

Ed climbed out of the car and ran into school.

In class, he tucked his feet under the desk so no one could see the shoes. But, at breaktime, he had to go **outside**.

RING!

There was nowhere to hide his feet in the yard, so he just had to stand there, with his baby buckles shining in the sun. He was sure that everyone was staring at him.

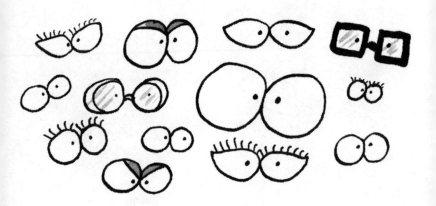

Paul and Steven were picking teams for football.

'I pick Conor,' said Paul.

'I pick Niall,' said Steven.

That was **everybody** – except Ed.

Paul and Steven weren't even
looking at him. They were looking at
his special shoes. They didn't pick
him. **Nobody** wanted to play with
someone in special shoes.

## CHAPTER 5

# When I was Young

Ed was **sulking** when Dad came home from his workshop.

Ed didn't say anything. You're not supposed to talk when you're sulking.

'Still upset about the shoes?' Dad asked, shaking sawdust out of his boots into the fire.

Ed couldn't answer, but he allowed himself a nod.

'Sometimes we **all** have to do things we don't want to, Ed. I remember when I was young ...'

Ed moaned. He wasn't in the mood for a story just now.

'Maybe I shouldn't tell you this story,' said Dad. 'It's pretty **horrible** ...'

Suddenly, Ed was interested. 'Oh, go on Dad. Tell me!'

'Okay,' said his father, 'when I was young, children often caught **worms**.'

'Children still dig up worms, Dad.'

'Oh no. I don't mean catch worms in the garden. I mean catch worms like you'd catch a cold.'

Ed's eyes opened wide. That was **disgusting**.

'If you drank dirty water, the worms could get into your tummy and eat all your dinner.'

'To get rid of these worms,' continued Dad, 'you had to drink a glass of **really revolting** medicine. But when I had worms, I didn't want to drink the medicine.'

'That's silly!' said Ed. 'Having medicine is better than having worms.'

'I know!' said Dad. 'But I was even younger than you, and I didn't understand that the medicine was for my own good.'

Ed nodded. He got the message.

Dad lifted Ed onto his knee.
'If I hadn't taken that medicine,
I'd have a worm as big as a
**snake** swimming around in my
belly today.'

Ed shivered. **Awful**.

Maybe Dad was right. **Maybe** he should wear the special shoes until his feet straightened out. But that doesn't make you feel any better, when you're not picked for the football team.

## CHAPTER 6

# Goal!!!

SPORTS' DAY

Friday was Sports' Day.
Mum dropped Ed off to
school.

'But, Mum,' he said,
'I won't even get picked for
football.'

Mum winked. 'Oh, I
think you will, Ed.
**Everybody** plays on
Sports' Day.'

Ed frowned. Mum was right.

Everyone had their best sports gear on. So did Ed. But his was ruined by the special shoes. What chance did he have against someone wearing trainers with special grips? **None**.

They lined up to pick football teams. Miss Byrne was in charge of the teams. She walked along the line, tapping everyone on the nose.

The 'ones' were in one team, and the 'twos' in the other.

Ed was a number one. **All** the other number ones groaned when he joined their group. This was terrible – worse than not being picked.

**No one** passed the ball to Ed.
He stood at the back of the field
staring at his special shoes.

'Come on, Ed!' said Miss Byrne.

'Come on, Ed!' shouted his Mum from the sideline.

But Ed didn't want to 'come on'. He wanted to go home and lock himself in his bedroom.

Then the ball bounced across the field and landed beside his foot.

Ed started to run. He wouldn't get very far. He never did. Any second now his turned-in feet would trip him up, and he would fall over.

But he didn't fall over. The special shoes kept his feet straight, and he kept going **all the way** up the field.

Mum was getting very excited,
jumping up and down.

'Come on, Ed! Come on, Ed!'

Ed ran faster and faster, kicking the ball in front of him. He ran so fast that no one could catch him. He ran right up to the **goal**, and whacked the ball as hard as he could. It went straight past the goalkeeper and into the net.

Miss Byrne blew the whistle,
and held up one finger.

Ed kept on running. He ran right over to Mum.

'Did you see me?' he asked.

'Yes I did,' smiled Mum.

'I didn't fall,' said Ed.

'I know,' said Mum. 'You were great. **Just brilliant**!'

'The special shoes. They kept my feet straight.'

Mum was so happy she had to blow her nose.

'You see. I told you ...'

'I know,' said Ed. 'They're for my own good.'

Mum lifted Ed up and swung him around. Ed **laughed** for the first time that week. He still didn't like the correction shoes, but he'd just have to get used to them. And so would everyone else.